Dear Parent:
Your child's love of reading starts here!

Every child learns to read in a different way and at his or her own speed. Some go back and forth between reading levels and read favorite books again and again. Others read through each level in order. You can help your young reader improve and become more confident by encouraging his or her own interests and abilities. From books your child reads with you to the first books he or she reads alone, there are I Can Read Books for every stage of reading:

SHARED READING
Basic language, word repetition, and whimsical illustrations, ideal for sharing with your emergent reader

BEGINNING READING
Short sentences, familiar words, and simple concepts for children eager to read on their own

READING WITH HELP
Engaging stories, longer sentences, and language play for developing readers

READING ALONE
Complex plots, challenging vocabulary, and high-interest topics for the independent reader

ADVANCED READING
Short paragraphs, chapters, and exciting themes for the perfect bridge to chapter books

I Can Read Books have introduced children to the joy of reading since 1957. Featuring award-winning authors and illustrators and a fabulous cast of beloved characters, I Can Read Books set the standard for beginning readers.

A lifetime of discovery begins with the magical words **"I Can Read!"**

Visit www.icanread.com for information on enriching your child's reading experience.

JUST CRITTERS WHO CARE

BY MERCER MAYER

HARPER

An Imprint of HarperCollinsPublishers

Braelynn Mercer Mayer has arrived!

Welcome, little Mayer, to your big family of
Critters Who Care!

Little Critter: Just Critters Who Care   Copyright © 2010 Mercer Mayer. All rights reserved. LITTLE CRITTER, MERCER
MAYER'S LITTLE CRITTER and MERCER MAYER'S LITTLE CRITTER and logo are registered trademarks of Orchard House
Licensing Company. All rights reserved. Manufactured in China. No part of this book may be used or reproduced in any manner
whatsoever without written permission except in the case of brief quotation embodied in critical articles and reviews. For information
address HarperCollins Children's Books, a division of HarperCollins Publishers, 10 East 53rd Street, New York, NY 10022.
www.icanread.com

Library of Congress Cataloging-in-Publication Data is available.
ISBN 978-0-06-083560-6 (trade bdg.) — ISBN 978-0-06-083559-0 (pbk.)

Typography by Diane Dubreuil
10   11   12   13   14   SCP   10 9 8 7 6 5 4 3 2 1
❖
First Edition

A Big Tuna Trading Company, LLC/J.R. Sansevere Book
www.littlecritter.com

I play ball at Tiger's house.
I hit the ball very hard.

The ball flies next door.

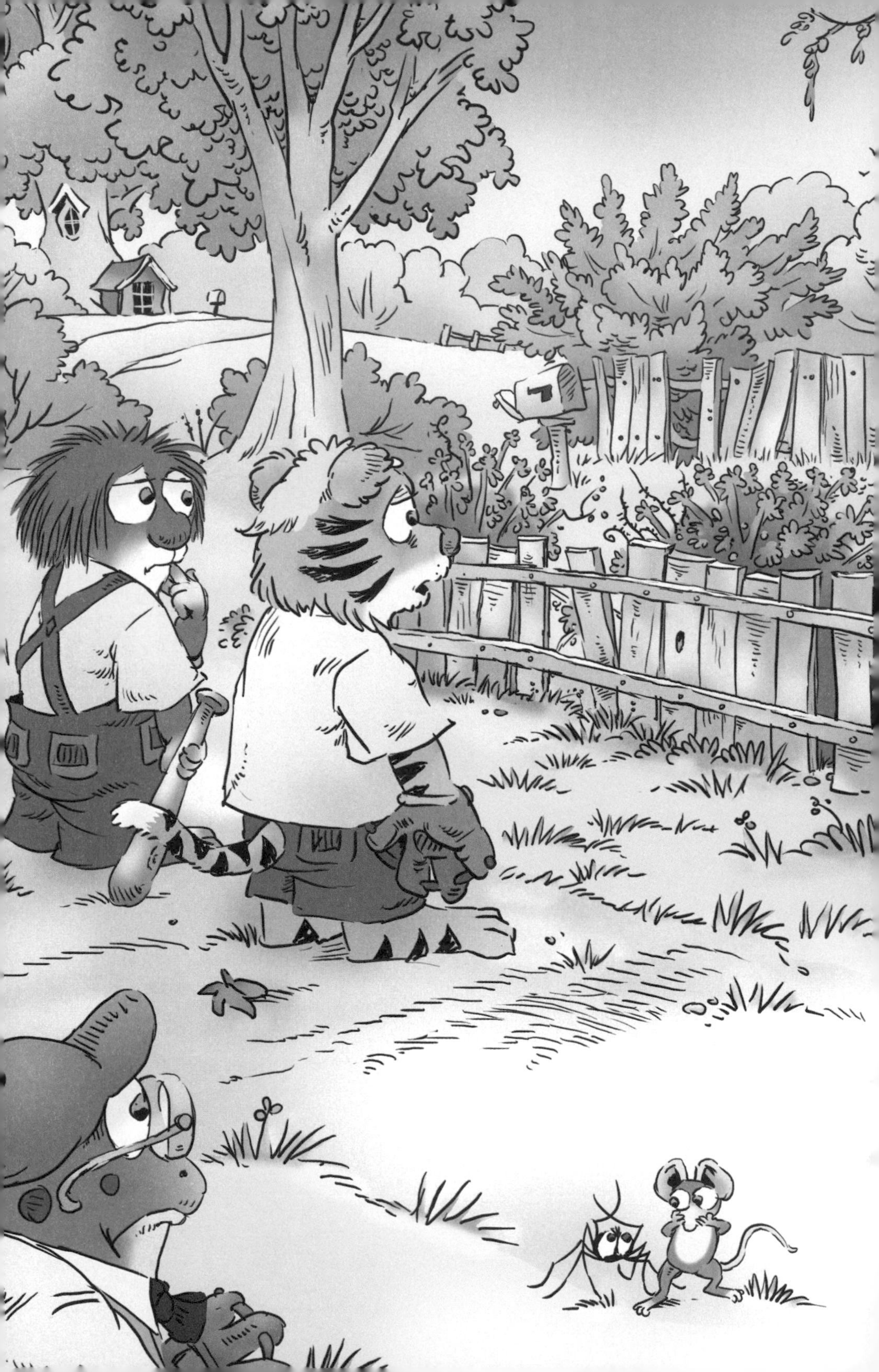

Uh-oh! The ball is in the spooky yard.

Maybe a monster lives there.

I am brave.

I will get the ball.

I run.

I trip and fall.

A little old bunny
hands me our ball.
"Thank you," I say.

"Tiger, there's no monster there," I say.

I ask my dad
why it looks so spooky
at the old bunny's house.

"Mrs. Bunny is not feeling well.

She has no one to help her," Dad say.

"We can help Mrs. Bunny.
We are critters who care," I say.

I call my friends.

"What a great idea.

We will help, too," they say.

I make a picture for T-shirts.

Little Sister helps.

Dad gets them made.

We meet at my house.

Everyone wears a T-shirt.

Parents come, too.

We all walk

to Mrs. Bunny's house.

I knock on the door.

Mrs. Bunny says, "Hello."

"We are Critters Who Care!

May we help you
with your yard?" I ask.
"Thank you," says Mrs. Bunny.

We clip the bushes.

We cut the grass.

We pull up weeds.
We trim the trees.

Dad fixes the porch step.

Tiger's dad fixes the shutter.

26

I blow away old leaves.

27

The house and yard look great!

Mrs. Bunny brings cookies
and juice for all.
I help carry them.

We say good-bye.
"What should we do next?"
I ask.

Little Sister says, "We can
get toys for kids
who don't have any."

Everyone says, "Good idea!"